USBORNE FIRST
Level

USBORNE FIRST READING

The
Gingerbread
Man

retold by
Mairi Mackinnon
Illustrated by Elena Temporin

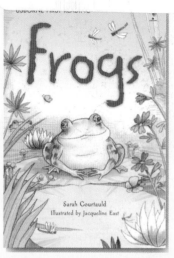

USBORNE FIRST READING

Frogs

Sarah Courtauld
Illustrated by Jacqueline East

USBORNE FIRST READING

The Goose
that laid the
Golden Eggs

based on the fable by
Aesop
Illustrated by
Daniel Howarth

USBORNE FIRST READING

The
ENORMOUS
TURNIP

based on the story by Alexei Tolstoy
Illustrated by Georgien Overwater

The Old Woman who swallowed a Fly

Illustrated by Sarah Horne

Edited by Kate Davies

Reading Consultant: Alison Kelly
Roehampton University

This is a story about
an old woman,

a fly,

a spider,

a bird,   a cat,

a dog,

a goat,

a cow

and
a horse.

There was an old
woman who swallowed
a fly.

I don't know why she
swallowed a fly.

Perhaps she'll die.

5

There was an old
woman who swallowed
a spider...

...that wriggled and
jiggled and tickled
inside her.

7

She swallowed the
spider to catch the fly.

I don't know why she
swallowed a fly.
Perhaps she'll die.

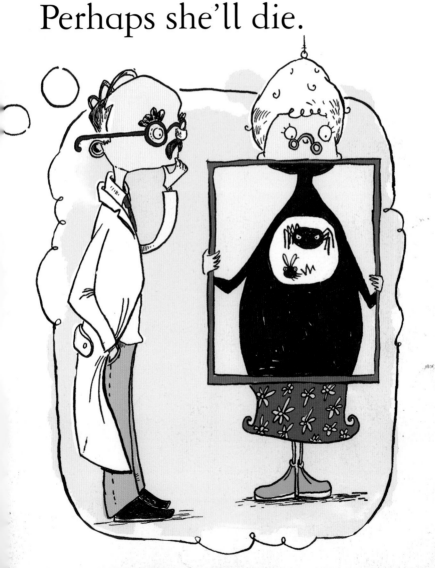

There was an old
woman who swallowed
a bird.

How absurd,
to swallow a bird!

11

She swallowed the bird
to catch the spider...

...that wriggled and
jiggled and tickled
inside her.

13

She swallowed the
spider to catch the fly.

14

I don't know why she
swallowed a fly.
Perhaps she'll die.

15

There was an old
woman who swallowed
a cat.

Imagine that,
to swallow a cat!

She swallowed the cat
to catch the bird.

She swallowed the bird
to catch the spider...

...that wriggled and
jiggled and tickled
inside her.

She swallowed the spider to catch the fly.

I don't know why she
swallowed a fly.

Perhaps she'll die.

There was an old
woman who swallowed
a dog.

What a hog, to
swallow a dog!

23

She swallowed the dog
to catch the cat.

She swallowed the cat
to catch the bird.

She swallowed the bird
to catch the spider...

...that wriggled
and jiggled and
tickled inside her.

27

She swallowed the
spider to catch the fly.

I don't know why she
swallowed a fly.
Perhaps she'll die.

There was an old
woman who swallowed
a goat.

Just opened her throat
to swallow a goat!

She swallowed the goat
to catch the dog.

She swallowed the dog
to catch the cat.

She swallowed the cat
to catch the bird.

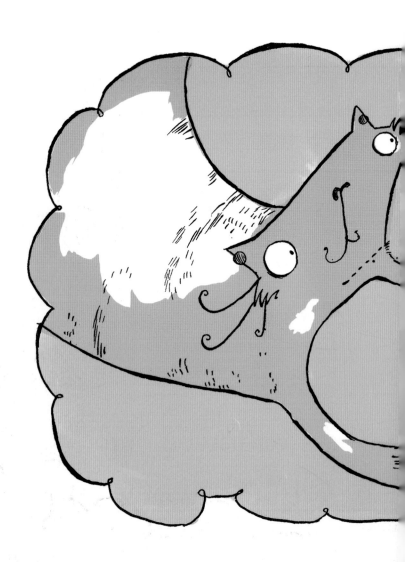

She swallowed the bird
to catch the spider...

...that wriggled and
jiggled and tickled
inside her.

36

She swallowed the
spider to catch the fly.

I don't know why she
swallowed a fly.
Perhaps she'll die.

There was an old
woman who swallowed
a cow.

I don't know how
she swallowed a cow!

She swallowed the cow
to catch the goat.

She swallowed the goat
to catch the dog.

She swallowed the dog
to catch the cat.

She swallowed the cat
to catch the bird.

She swallowed the bird
to catch the spider...

...that wriggled
and jiggled and
tickled inside her.

She swallowed the
spider to catch the fly.

I don't know why she
swallowed a fly.
Perhaps she'll die.

There was an old
woman who swallowed
a horse.

She's dead, of course!

Designed by Caroline Spatz
Series designer: Russell Punter
Series editor: Lesley Sims
Digital manipulation: John Russell

First published in 2008 by Usborne Publishing Ltd., Usborne House,
83-85 Saffron Hill, London EC1N 8RT, England. www.usborne.com
Copyright © 2008 Usborne Publishing Ltd.

48

USBORNE FIRST READING
Level Four

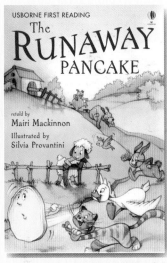

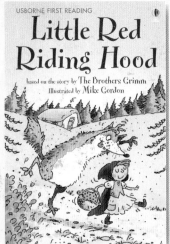